ROCKFORD PUBLIC LIBRARY
3 1112 020293425

D1573288

For my beloved teacher
Dr. Seyyed Hossein Nasr.
~AYL

For all the animals, for as Mahatma Gandhi said,
"The greatness of a nation and its moral progress
can be judged by the way its animals are treated." ~Demi

When the Animals Saved Earth: An Eco-Fable

Wisdom Tales is an imprint of World Wisdom, Inc.

The illustrations are rendered in mixed media.

Book Design by Stephen Williams
Printed in China on acid-free paper
Production Date: November 2014
Plant & Location: Printed by 1010 Printing International Ltd
Job / Batch #: TT14080904
For information address Wisdom Tales,
P.O. Box 2682, Bloomington, Indiana 47402-2682
www.wisdomtalespress.com

LIBRARY OF CONGRESS CATALOGING-IN-PUBLICATION DATA
Lumbard, Alexis York, 1981-
When the animals saved Earth : an eco-fable / retold by Alexis York Lumbard ; illustrated by Demi.
pages cm
Includes note about the history of the tale.
ISBN 978-1-937786-37-3 (hardcover : alk. paper)
I. Demi, illustrator. II. Ikhwan al-Safa'. Rasa'il. 21. English. III. Title.
PZ7.L978714Whe 2015 [E]--dc23 2014040811111

Author's Note

This book was inspired by a 1,000-year-old fable with a fascinating, multi-faith history. The first version, *The Case of the Animals Versus Man Before the King of the Jinn*, was written in Arabic by the Muslim Brethren of Purity and appeared in 10th-century Iraq. The tale then traveled all the way to 14th-century Europe, where the Christian King Charles I of Hungary had Rabbi Kalonymus ben Kalonymus translate the story into Hebrew and Latin. The Hebrew version remained popular in Jewish communities until the early 20th century. Recently, it has been revived, in English, as *The Animals Lawsuit Against Humanity*, by Rabbi Anson Laytner and Rabbi Dan Bridge (Fons Vitae, 2005). It is to this version that I owe much gratitude. As with previous versions, mine too takes poetic liberties: in particular, the figure of Adam was largely inspired by another classical Islamic fable, *Hayy Ibn Yaqzan*.

When the Animals Saved Earth

An Eco-Fable

Retold by

Alexis York Lumbard

Illustrated by

Demi

A gem of an island glimmered in the bright, blue sea. Here the winged and webbed, hoofed and horned, mighty and meek, all lived in peace.

They did so under the quiet watch of King Bersaf. He was a spirit king, made of fire and air.

The creatures of
Emerald Isle knew
nothing of humans,
for none had come to
their shores.

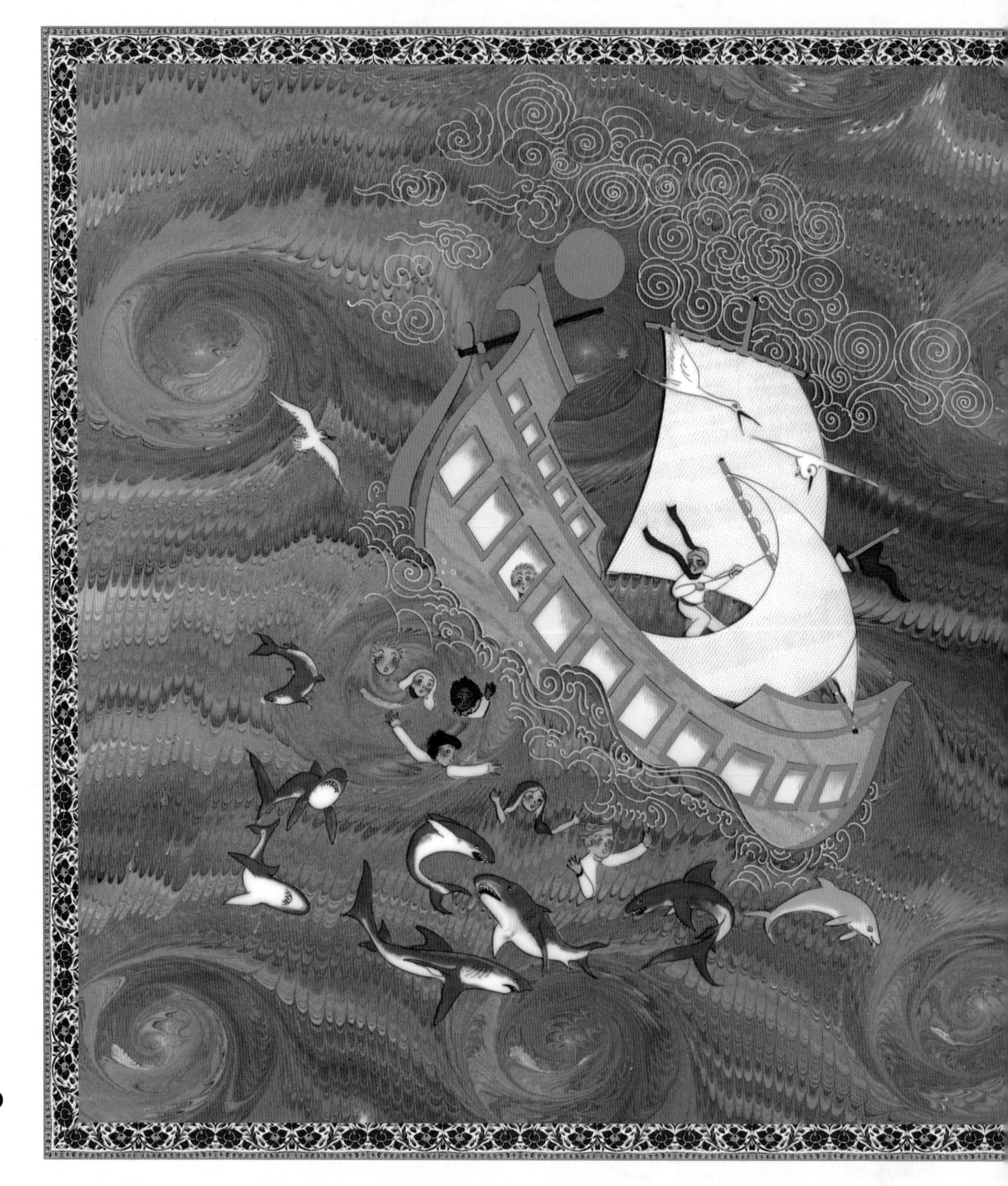

But one morning,
after a terrible storm,
the winds of fate
blew an ark full of
people their way.

How quickly the island changed! Down came trees and up went homes.

Soon there were farms and a bustling market where all the people gathered.

Everyone, that is, but a young boy named Adam.
He had little interest in the ways of the people.

Instead, he spent his days skipping stones and watching waves. Best of all, he loved swimming with the sea turtles.

But other people wanted more and more. “If I had an ox,” said one, “it could plow me a field twice as large.” “Yes,” chuckled another. “A strong beast would make me rich!” “Hats,” added a woman, “how I miss those feathered hats.”

“Grab your weapons!” the men shouted, marching to the jungle.

How unsuspecting were the poor beasts! Only a few managed to escape.

Those that remained were shackled in chains and dragged to the market.

The night was filled with a chorus of the animals' tears. "I can't bear it!" sighed Adam with a heavy heart. So he sneaked out of his window and crept into the forest.

Before long a lion appeared. “Don’t worry,” he cautioned. “I am not here to eat you.” “You can speak?” replied Adam in surprise. “Yes,” said the lion. “But only a pure heart can understand me.”

“Why did you run away from home?” asked the lion. “I wanted to help,” answered Adam. “Well,” said the lion, “follow me. We might need you.”

In a secret meadow, the free animals waited. "Gather round," roared the lion. "It is time to summon King Bersaf." So all the animals squawked and squealed, howled and hissed, panted and roared. Adam joined in too. Suddenly, a cloud of mist appeared.

"Who makes the ancient circle
And draws me from the Peak?
Here I am, your King Bersaf,
So name yourselves and speak!"

"Your Majesty, it is I, the lion. We seek your help." And he spoke to King Bersaf of the great sadness in the land.

The king nodded,

"Weep no more, my mighty son,
For on the morning light
Man and beast will meet in court
To hear your sorry plight."

"Adam," said King Bersaf, *"Return to town, and gather your people. I wish to speak with them."*

At the court of King Bersaf the humans stood wide-eyed and frozen. **Thump! Thump! Thump!** went the old wooden staff.

"O human folk, please answer now
This charge of rule by fear.
The beasts say you do great harm
Throughout my Emerald Sphere."

A man of proud appearance spoke. “Your Majesty, these animals fuss over nothing. We treat them fine.”

“Fine!” brayed the donkey. “Look at my bones! Do they look fine to you?”

"And what about the chickens?" continued the donkey. "You stuff my friends into tiny cages without a single blade of grass!"

“Even greater horrors take place, but tender ears are near.”

"Humans, what do you say for yourselves?" demanded King Bersaf.

"What does it matter?" said another. "Why, look at all the good that we do. We build. We make. Without us there would be no order to this wild island."

"Nonsense!" screeched the owl. "You chop down the forests, dirty the skies, and poison the waters! This is destruction, not order!"

“Hear! Hear!” cheered the ant. “My people are also great builders, creating miles of magnificent tunnels. We do this for ourselves, but we also give.”

“We care for our young and old. We turn the soil. We spread the seeds. We are givers. But not the humans. From what we can see, all you do is take. And hurt. Have you no shame?”

“No shame?” lashed back the people. “How dare you!”

And they all began to shout. Human against animal. Animal against human. Adam stood to the side, his eyes closed and his heart aching.

Thump! Thump! Thump! went the old wooden staff. King Bersaf spoke.

"This case against the humans
Is rather plain and clear.
They are guilty of spreading
Destruction, wrong, and fear.

And only in compassion,
When human hearts do feel
The impact of their actions
Will Emerald Isle heal."

With a final thump, King Bersaf withdrew from the animals the pain they were carrying. Then he took that pain and scattered it among the humans. In their hearts they would now feel as the animals did. And then King Bersaf vanished.

With heads hung low, the humans returned to town. And all the beasts, with faces glowing bright and Adam by their side, returned to the jungle. Little by little, the healing began.

A gem of an island glimmered in the deep, blue universe. And what a special island it was! For here the winged and webbed, hoofed and horned, mighty and meek, lived in hopeful peace. It was their one and only home and they called it EARTH.

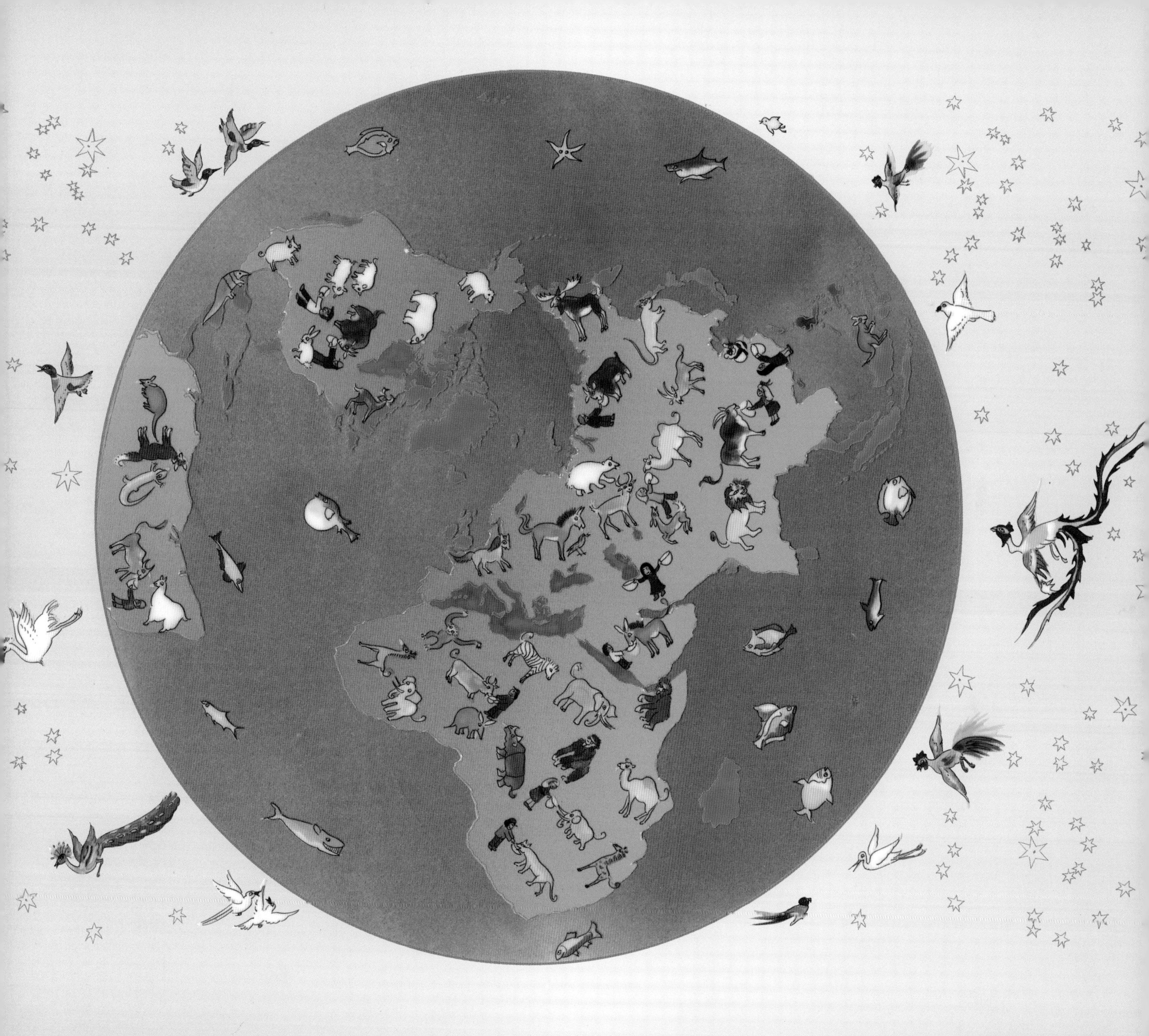